"Genius is nothing more nor less
than childhood recaptured at will."

— Charles Baudelaire,
(from "The Painter of Modern Life" 1863)

Also by Fabrice Poussin

In Absentia (Silver Bow Publishing 2021)

IF I HAD A GUN

by

Fabrice Poussin

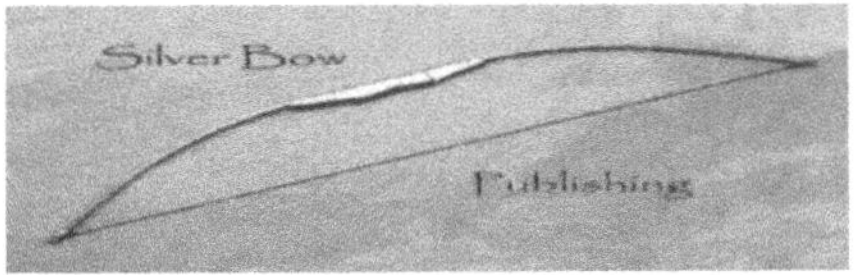

Silver Bow Publishing
720 Sixth Street, Box # 5
New Westminster, BC
CANADA   V3L3C5

Title: If I Had a Gun
Author: Fabrice Poussin
Cover Art: "November Beach"
Cover Design: Candice James
Layout and Editing: Candice James
ISBN: 9781774032350(print)
ISBN: 9781774032367 (e-book)

ISBN: 9781774032350 Print
ISBN: 9781774032367 eBook
© 2022 Silver Bow Publishing

Library and Archives Canada Cataloguing in Publication

Title: If I had a gun / by Fabrice Poussin.
Names: Poussin, Fabrice, author.
Description: Poems.
Identifiers: Canadiana (print) 20220406405 | Canadiana (ebook) 20220406421 | ISBN 9781774032350
   (softcover) | ISBN 9781774032367 (Kindle)
Classification: LCC PS3616.O875 I5 2022 | DDC 811/.6—dc23

5

**To my students
may they continue imagining, persist in creating
and never stop dreaming.**

If I Had a Gun

CONTENTS

If I Had a Gun

If I had a gun
it would have nine chambers
one made of chocolate and another
of caramel.

If I had a weapon like that
I would dip it in a white cream
made of whipped butter
and powdered sugar.

If I owned a revolver
it would sing with every shot
a melody made in Heaven
every night before I dream.

If I hid an instrument of death in my bedroom
I would devour it with strawberries
and smile with every bite
at that silly lady with a scythe.

But you will find nothing of the sort
in my humble abode
unless of course you think of ice cream
as a deadly nectar.

90-Year-Old Trickster

Bright wheels shine upon the green linoleum
intermittently singing a song of rust and thirst
within the deafening silence of a thick smog.

Eyes sharp as a fox seeking his next prey
he believes in a flight to the freedom next door.

Those lines on a leathery visage attest to the smiles
recalling witnesses to the many pranks suffered
a story yet to continue for this 90-year-old trickster.

Halls like a labyrinth, but not a prison yet,
as he roams between walls, as he does in his thoughts
playing the same game he invented when still a child.

A mysterious smile hovers on the mischievous lips
of this wheelchair speed racer up to his old tricks.

Murmuring a brief song of commonplace clichés
is his warning to those who dare stay in his way
that soon they will be caught in the laughter he made for them.

He may not remember the decades spent reeling
nor the time of day or the seasons in the orchard
yet he rules in this kingdom, 90-year-old king of tricksters.

A Bed Under the Rains

Thundering rains on the steel covers
bright streaks across the walls of shadows
and the loud crash below the leafy oak.

Heat of a summer day in early spring
the sky falls apart at first sign of exhaustion
darkness secedes under sabers of a last sun.

Softly she rests, her gaze set on a glassy sheet,
dreaming of a dance in the dead of night
energized by the lights of a puzzling heaven.

If only she could read the song of those tears
smell the kindest caress of a whiter cloud
she wonders as she touches her aching essence.

Beacon in the Stone

Predicted darkness set on the laborious hour
thick as stone, cold as infinity.

Still now, hands crossed upon his breath
he recalls heavy days of unbearable Augusts.

Gaze set on a sterile imitation of heaven
he finds no message of things to come.

The gifts of yesteryear reassigned
he may now ponder the dearest present.

A particle small as an atom shines above,
the unsuspected home for everything he was.

The body sleeps now but his mind wanders
into eternities made of entangled dreams.

The light is the string that will take him
against time through the ages of the universe.

Broken Bones

Don't fall, don't cry, and please don't worry
the evening meal flavors the great domain
rain hammers at the glass, sparks in the stove
little boy can taste the delicacies of evening.

School is done for the day, homework will come
then sleep in the cozy down bed, close to the door
almost to ensure escape from the second floor
warm, fragrance of old forgotten aromas.

The chair is high, near the dinner table
little and frail, ancient as he can see
she is as a ballerina juggling with balance
is it worthwhile for an old tin can?

The dish is not from home, like on vacation
a stone's throw from there, of love and care
she knows what he likes, she never fails
perhaps she too dreamed of this today.

Early she went to the garden, she peeled, she cooked
she sowed, and she cleaned, and swept, and forgot
to rest her old frail bones, one by one screaming
as help would not come, did not come.

She gave him his blood, and much more in her love
rarely her lips smiled, but she had to know ...
she had to know what happiness she made
when she saw his big black eyes devour her meal.

Cannoli and Cupcakes

Sitting, away from snow, sleet, ice, and cold snaps
there is only one thing left for him, spectator of
the lives never to be his, vicariously through the glass.

Eyes closed, inhaling the nearby world in one breath
ignoring giggles, laughter, screams and cash registers' melodies,
he leans back in his temporary sphere, in the corner.

The massive door opens wide, boy and girl in first, for they know
the sweet flavor of a tummy soon filled by the flavor
of glazed pastries, while mom and dad drink their little joy.

Tiny goals of renewed happiness', simple days of twins
year after year, birthdays of every day, Christmas again
to many of all sizes, heaven for a moment with friends.

The universe stands still, near Broadway, so far away yet
the family returns to the heat of the home hearth
leaving behind them a heart for followers to share.

It is an ongoing line of lives, seeking their well-earned peace
joys on the in, joy there, and again on the out, pure joy
a house of cupcakes to forget every hurt always.

Chameleon

Chameleon girl in her father's working boots
playing with a brother's construction set of steel
she giggles on the wooden floor full of chards
under the glassy look of her friendly doll in pink.

Chameleon woman walks on the avenue
perfect in her stilettos bright as night
legs wrapped in black silk under the business skirt
eager for the worn-out sweats and a daily Havana.

Chameleon man at the office with the guys
trapped in his three-piece daydreaming a gentler life
anxious for that moment of return to his laboratory
scissors and the delights of creating new dress designs.

Chameleon boy I might play with the girls today
banning the colorful images of those famous jocks
relax in the tender embrace of my joyful self
and sleep in the ecstasy of their confusion.

I am them living in the great palace of my soul
fortunate for the gift they have made to this body
free to choose how I will spend another day
entire in the aloneness everyone fears.

Dante Dream

Waking up with Dante at 3 am
chairs of purple velvet in a dark room
damp with the smell of formaldehyde.

Friends stood in need of a last embrace
blue of a waxy substance chalky as death
forgotten carcasses on a country road.

They spoke not a word, moved not an inch
clones of a single self, statues to yesterdays
their stench overpowering all that lives.

The air frigid with infinite darkness before the door
to be taken soon upon the dreaded hour
for it was too late to return to living.

Fluttering with your Butterflies

The room is vast and empty
with only her facing the tall glass
standing she teases her hair once more
peace seems to surround her.

Still then, she wonders as she dives
into her own soul, tingling inside
her soft hand touching the womb
a slight sigh, a smile, and a memory.

In the corner, lost in this immensity
of barren walls, a window so far
a door unattainable; in the distance
solidity fades, colors vanish.

Tall, thin, in a light gown of stars and fairy dust
apparition, a breeze heaves the adored breast
her curls play hide and seek behind her lobes
tickle the shoulders; she tilts her head.

Another brush stroke, the lids wink in the mirror
she knows the presence is near, tingles again
her eyes close, the arms press against her sides
the breath is of pleasure, it is of life, hers, simply.

Freezing the World

We are told it is awfully cold out there in space
a realm of a myriad questions in the stars
but tonight, I froze the world, if but for a moment.

This universe took on the shape it chose of its own
sparkles here, lines there, and a crevasse of two
streams, rivers, and oceans came to a standstill.

It became visible, whole in all its intimacy
and it was mine then, to see, to own and understand
through its glassy mirror, its icy infinite shroud.

Kaleidoscopic perception fixed forever on the plane
offering colors of blacks and whites, and billions more
alive in an apparent image of final death.

Universes galore from all angles, without order
nor geometry, nor physics, simply suspended in immensity
reflection of a soul I am still attempting to discover.

I froze the world tonight, and for the first time
I caught a true image of who I was meant to be
another astronaut, traveler in time and space for all eternity.

Half Past Eternity

It may have been past a millennium
in a space where time was futile.

A spec in the vast darkness or perhaps
a galaxy swirling through the unknown.

Alive it moved with the grace of a dancer
wearing stars for its only adornment.

It thought in a way mysterious to this realm
yet it sought the matter to seal eternity.

On its quest for a most common dream
fully aware of what was written.

Upon a blue world, it became just like them
to sit in wait of what had been foretold.

A strange miracle shared by another
born to a race so unfamiliar.

There on the corner, of a coffee shop
contact and an eternal journey to pursue.

Fatal to the flesh foreign to the visitor's
to save her, it was to take her away.

Energy never created and not to vanish
it took her in and made her a part of itself.

Now they travel an unlikely odyssey
without reason, only true to the cosmos.

In a Fiery Sea

I swam through a sea of flames
giddy as the dolphin in friendly waves
gliding inside the currents of history.

It was morning perhaps or even darkness
in the fiery ocean of a gentle embrace.

This day anew I will dive to oblivion
to burn and form melodic phrases of light
as once centuries disappeared into thin smog.

The memory of this frail body within another
as in the ashes of Pompeii with many lives to live.

Unscathed again the bones will emerge
to make a new skin, a semi-God to celebrate
the eternal mother, sister, lover of all dawns.

Landscape

I touched the peak of Mont Blanc to sense it shiver
its eternal snows thawing for a brief instant.

I saw its water flow into torrents of life
as I longed to taste the purity of a first bath.

Roaming the valleys, rolling hills, and many hollows
I pondered the warmth of a rising sun in the dew.

Meadows spawn in deserts forgotten, fertile
eager to bring life exploding as on the first dawn.

Oceans await in unconceivable patience
cyclones and typhoons hover their ghastly shapes.

What will you say when you awaken to the scene
gently slumbering in a landscape to your image?

Gazes will meet, two souls will join in dreams
twins again in awe of an admiring galaxy.

Once a City

I traveled through the old zone
in the gown of former evenings
thinking myself an amazon warrior.

Darkness ruled in the early dawn
held by the stronghold of mistaken dreams
I walked against the storm on icy pavements.

Skeletons of ancient lives surrounded my breath
trying to capture the essence of my breast
threatening with their oozing darkness.

The ghosts of those distant pasts assaulted my bones
trembling within the paleness of their fears
so, the eyes of desolate murals spied upon my days.

I could see no glass in the broken visions
only gaping memories of deathly sorrows
appealing to my remaining hours for salvation.

I continued on the desert paths of the city
seeking the beat of another life only
to fall on my knees on the edge of an abyss.

Song of a Butterfly

She awoke early in the warmth of July
shedding the cocoon of her tender home
to take flight upon the currents of summer.

Hours preparing to match her awesome sister
she painted colors on her ephemeral wings
sighing in a last effort to break free.

There is no time for second thoughts
when the mountain calls for one of its children
to join in and make her world complete.

She is an Adonis Blue as the stellar realms
seeking her Purple Emperor in the falling hours
she sings a soft flutter to the distant woods.

Too far away to be known, her voice reaches
a mate gifted with timeless patience and
together in a sweet murmur they will embrace.

As if in the heart of a myriad fireflies
they will bring a new star to the heavens
and peacefully sleep in the silence of her song.

Broken Pinocchio

They make sounds like bags of marbles
moving along on certain paths
seeking evasive grooves filled with blood.

Their dislocated hearts, houses of cards
fragile under the breeze of heaven
resonate with the echoes of distant ruins.

Waltzing a mad dance between a death and a dream
they may reach to an unseen evil in the blue
swatting at invincible blades of a hazy glow.

Mounted on the strings of a blind executioner
they are puppets flowing with a black potion
ready to fall prisoners of a master atop a great mount.

Mechanical engines born of a passionate spark
juicy robots on their quest for an anchor
they fail in becoming the image of a father.

Jerking through dubious roads of unfinished lives
they stumble on infinite particles of forfeited futures
never quite living, icy with death in a blaring sun.

Ragged dolls at the hands of their vengeful gods
condemned to pursue the dance of shattered shadows
as many Sisyphus desperate for a safe exit.

Broken sorrows of a toy named Pinocchio
they will forever roam the deadly avenues of destinies
leading into a thickening darkness to oblivion.

Crimson Blade

25

Must the blade be of crimson shades
for the lady to feel safe in the cold tower?

Should the steed be of noble white
to find his way home to the gentle squire?

Will the magicians of the deep forest
stay put in their dens while waiting for their dwarves?

Why is the quest for adventure to the death
when must one remain to mend so many scars?

What will the maiden find beneath the armor
but a hollow chest abandoned of the lion's heart!

Can the blade not keep its pristine spark
for the kingdom to be the safe heaven she sought?

Home at Last

It was so very easy
to empty the teal urn
twixt the twin trees.

Mornings have come and gone,
frosts have thawed away
and the scorching sun has
again cooked your grounds.

In a bed of fallen sheets
you sleep, pieces of soul,
ashes to ashes, and just that.

A neighbor frowns upon
your very presence, at home,
nosy as the ancestors taught.

Your name on a granite rock,
smooth, in concrete, left there,
a place to come and salute you.

We tuck you in once again,
a last gaze at your little heaven,
and a good-by, until next time when
a family we will become anew.

If Ever I Were to Die

If ever I were to die, I would take the whole world with me
and leave just enough so everyone would recall
there was once a tree of sweet cherries in the midst of the city.

If ever I were to forget, I would carve my name in stone
and stand vigil above the growing moss and lichens
as once did the philosopher haunted by his memories.

If ever you were to walk the path still warm without regrets
and slow as you pondered in the ever lightness of your dress
just as in your dreams you often fancied such a saunter.

If ever they might take a moment to inhale the spheres
and listen to the pounding of their dying hopes
perhaps they would hear the answers to their cries.

If ever we were to fly to traverse the realms above Mt Blanc
merely dressed of a gentle snow blown by the breath of infinity
might you gaze and shut your mind to the world below?

If ever I were to live, I would not bother so much to land
and search for an anchor, trite safety of unsuspected danger
I would let my spirit glide and softly encounter its mate.

Kid

Never grew up
the little farmer boy
under a rough shell of a man
rugged and hard at work.

A little farmer boy
skin so thick with weather
old cuts barely healed
under new signatures of time.

What happened to pain
and to tiredness?
Little farmer boy
had not a moment!

Hands obeyed the heart
legs followed the soul
and once in a while
the sweetness of a breath.

Barely clothed enough
in a cold snap of winter
mittens somewhere forgotten
and the roar of the engine.

Eyes so sharp to the horizon
full of a light without end
never losing sight of the goal
bringing warmth all around.

The little farmer boy
never grew up, never grew old
his heart beats with God
his soul marches with Angels.

Panam

Papa cries in his old, rugged beard, while Gertrude holds his hand;
they think of Ben and Tom, and Ezra, and Josephine, and Scott
if only they could join forces with the living of the street
they too would walk and hold fires of hope.

Under the Saint by the river gray and sad, no man fishes
the bookstalls have nothing to say, their secrets they will keep
silence prevails, and the flashing lights have given up
numbers by the hour have been thrown; no one knows.

Dizzie, Duke, Louis, Dexter, will you please play us a tune
you know, your deep, unwritten songs from your old souls
you see, I can tell you are on the verge of endless tears
this tore you apart a little more in your tight grave.

The city, old girl, grown, abused, and raped once again
is not alone. There is an army on the rise, one unseen
ghosts so many, of all sizes, makes, colors, and feeling
awakened, they are intent on the task theirs.

From memory of two millennia and more, the heart will beat
anew, stronger at the footsteps of one hundred million souls
a shockwave infinite, sending tremors to all parts, electric
it will be felt to the end of the galaxy, to the universe entire.

God will not rest, moved by the resurrection of the forgotten ones
for a dagger has pierced the creation again, a little more deeply now
it turns and twists inside a wound it wants gangrenous, incurable
the pain is immeasurable, the hurt intense, it is not yet death.

Bodies scream, they agonize, some succumb, and families die
the wave of hate grows wider, travels great distances into space
time echoes with the cracking sounds of the last breaths on the
asphalt never to be forgotten, imprinted in the heavenly memory.

This morning the blood has run with the early rain to feed the sea
those with hopes under the white shroud have found their last home

the city weeps, her veins filled with a strange substance
it is time to rest, my beloved, Papa watches, will tuck you in.

Pretty girl of centuries, playful, glorious in colors and song
sleep this day. Let the nightmare settle, your friends are many
Papa will hold you when you wake, he will lead you to your people
know that the world is your lover, and never will betray you.

Good old Hem, hanging with Scott, a little too drunk, a bit too boyish
they walk the riverbanks, greet the bum, speak of Gotham
chase the dog enamored with the American lingo, young
Paris, their girl shared, they just want to go fishing again.

Remembering Toulouse

It has been another night in the corner
watching a distant crowd inches away
deafened by the constant din of the darkness.

She cannot recall the stroll in the mist
against the blinding eyes of steel monsters
as again she sits alone nursing her priceless poison.

Dressed in the patches of her private treasures
she seems a stranger in a smoky cloud
surrounded by the thunderous clamors of the mob.

Statuesque in the pose of a scared child
a halo shapes her uncertain presence
she stares in search of another world.

She is the void left after the ghost has vanished
frigid within the burning smog that was once her
everything and defines the essence of others.

Rue de Fleurus

Words, commas, sentences seemingly incomplete
grumpy lady ageless lost in a sea of paintings
sitting on the same old chair, like a master builder.

Architect of a new age, syllables became bricks
cemented by chance into a kaleidoscope of voices
inspiration of a broken time with solidly shut doors.

Rough old lady wearing dresses of worn-out burlap
pulling no punches for the unsuspecting wannabe
surrounded by the energy of a generation.

Sizing them all up as they walked in for tea and talked
so few knew of the true depth of an unfathomable heart
still found every day in the old apartment on Fleurus.

No ghost haunts those streets for none is large enough
to carry with it the legacy of the colossal marble Venus;
on the contrary it is you to be found on every corner.

Fragments of a life everywhere, from Appalachia to the lights
cubist in your soul, with your words, as you appear still
piece by piece you are more wholesome than wholeness could be.

Sing my dear, your dislocated lines, with the voices
of automobile engines broken down, lost on a country road
your voice echoes through the ages and warms our rhymes.

The Old Man and the World

Late one evening he walked out into life again
perhaps not his, as the world seemed abandoned
the thin mist penetrated the rags he called a coat
the last remnants of the dream of a kingdom.

I saw him holding his riches in his hand like a globe
warm as if a part of those ancient pieces of a self
a glow transpired in a dense reddish hue.

I saw him clasping his soul to his breast
carefree in the silence of another quiet eve
a few more steps to vanish into his personal darkness.

I saw him cherishing a heart as if his only treasure
one beating softly, the child of unfortunate hopes
his eyes weary of a false step to a fatal stumble.

I think I saw him sheltering his love
in a makeshift fortress so close to his chest;
he continued on his solitary path into his story.

I know I saw him writing his life with blood
so warm with the fire of undisclosed passions;
leaving many deaths behind he went on so stoic
still seeking to carve upon space memories not yet made.

Thirteen Wrinkles

They walk, proud, jolly, almost handsome
thirteen wrinkles, and two double-chins
one is fifteen feet across, the other like a ball
rolls down to the eating spot early morning.

An eighteen-months old toddler cries in
the octogenarian's diaper at the registrar;
shorty punches keys without looking
and baldy is getting impatient with his gun.

Lucky the politician is there bellowing on the P.A.
five inches deep and six high, he smokes too much
can't scratch that itch behind his left brain
his left arm too screams with the extended tattoo.

Long necks, and short, stubby faces and girlish
ants in a farm under the spy glass, they run
headless, armless, thoughtless, meandering
in a life that may be theirs, and then again...

Upon a Dream

I walked through the hours
wrapped in the shroud of simple days
cold in the middle of August's melting rays.

Hope seemed far removed
on an avenue of dark towers and strangers
trying to avoid the blades of December ice.

The city of many hostile gazes
an eerie reality of imperfect ghosts;
a foe growing into a bizarre black paste.

Refuge exists in oblivion
when sleep will come at last a sedative
to the crushing pains of a mere stroll.

There, a miracle
a life imagined by random chance
immune from the rules of the streets.

Drained by the demands upon her
she too explores the infinite possibilities
to enter the domain of her own relativity.

Upon my embrace she trusts her breath
her eyes closed she no longer trembles
safe again as she travels to eternal truth.

Cradled by the Milky Way

This night the universe is my cradle;
in his hands I recline and slumber
smiling soul in the comfort of the giant.

Gently rocked on the waves of ages
of light, dark filaments, and clouds
I might not sleep another instant.

The ocean of black, filled with stars
paradox to what is known, only seen
it is no hiding place for the grand truth.

I escape unnoticed, slipping from this home
somber, under the centenary oaks
night-owl, at ease into the great abyss.

Time is an ally confused by eternal hours
fused to the depth of space, boundless,
the galaxy is my true cradle and
I will never close my eyes again.

On the Walls of the Old Fort

Khaki shorts may not suffice
to make the dream of a war complete.

Toy guns shaped of fallen tree limbs
and popping sounds from the mouths of babes.

Distant images of boys and girls at play
on a battlefield once of blood red rivers.

Pondering the last days of a scorching summer
an aged visitor leans upon a curvy stick.

Scanning an endless panorama eyes closed
the old warrior recalls confused memories.

Summer dresses, sandals with flowery giggles
and the surprise of a gentle fall in blades of grass.

Stumbling with a deathly thump into a muddy pool
surrounded by the darkness of many a running mate.

Still on the prairie, the flaneur feels a teasing breeze as
tears explode upon the face where once peace had a home.

Child again, child at last, innocent of a genderless youth
cries for the hours of well-being on the tragedies
still echoing within the walls of the old fort.

Killers of Dreams

A little prince in broken-down shoes
he did not know what royalty might be
living below the moats of the old citadel
dwelling under a slab of mud and bark
sleeping of the dreams of sweet babes.

His deep blues opened wide in the morning dew
looking up to the mirror of his soul, he smiled
fingers deep into the bottomless pockets
remembering the marbles lost days before
treasures filled his little chest with snickers.

He would be king some day and live up above
like his father before him, in a royal shack
made for a fisherman without a pole
a warrior without armor, leaking pearls
from clouds which cried tears of joy for him.

No prison to be built for the sprouting imagination
or boundaries for a love greater than his whole kin's
in awe they will soon raise a wondering gaze
when he takes flight to another world he made
and asks whence his immense power came.

A little sorry, as alone in numbers they must remain
the dream killers cannot survive the enchantment
searching stone and brick, to build fortresses
isolated, safe from the threat of possible awe
their prince, free, cries for them, for it is too late.

Dress of Stone

Year last it was in sheen steel that she waltzed
across the cosmic spheres.

Bright of silverfish blue, the garment swam
within the waves of galaxies.

Pearls burst in quiet verses as she twirled
into a neighboring trance.

Locked beyond the fragments of icy chapters
timid inside the fortress.

Forever in motion at the rhythm of many suns
she fled through an awesome realm.

Hovering above the ramparts of other lives
when it was of stone, she made her dress.

Amazon, gentle as the newborn seraphim
never free from the gazes and touches of man.

A dress of mail fragile as crystal
vulnerable to all the abounding dangers.

In her misty shroud, safe at last, like an ether
she pirouettes with the gaiety of great deity.

The Discarded

What must he do with the rests of an unfinished life
to whom can the wanderer bequeath another quest
alone, gazing at infinite tomorrows he may never know?

Much pavement lies on the path so often trodden
worn with cracks of unending earthquakes
there is no chance he may double back.

Weary of luggage heavy with wasted memories
the aging shoulders tire of yet another highway
the words fail as the last echoes of lost cares.

The path continues forward to unsoundable obscurity
for him to sublimate in a dimension of loneliness
there will be no regrets in a soul without anchor.

The last chest may be found abandoned
fallen victim to the next generation of dying hearts
bearing the singular message "Just Get Rid of It"
in the awkward last river of his blood.

Another Earth

Thinking herself a reborn Da Vinci
she gathers the precious mud
a little ball between the juvenile palms.

Upon the arid dune of ancient peaks
she ponders the heavy flash from above
a mirage hovering the soft crests.

Her gaze above a soft shoulder
she touches her burning skin
brown with the sunset hours.

Considering the globe within her will
she makes a planet to many treasures
a tingling reaching her entrails.

It is a grail offered to a new dusk
the gift she will reserve for a stranger
conqueror of unknown realms.

She fashions the home to her dreams
soft mounds upon luscious valleys
shapes she knows well from infancy.

Now she may close her eyes
at peace at the edge of final darkness
floating on the curves of her birth.

My DMZ

Never was I in a war
to see the bombs kiss the fields
changing the plains of green
to everlasting sparks of red.

Yet every day I travel
through an almost forgotten world
boards on the eyes of old histories
scars in the ground where man once lived.

I drive in the safety of my tank
eyeing to old military jargons
through a periscope and night vision goggles
slowly, a spectator more than a fighter.

Little is left of hopes and dreams now razed
castles of clapboards and found blocks of mountains
they echo of lives left vacant amid sadness
I have visions of DMZs on the late news shows.

A futuristic landscape of apocalyptic films
surrealistic images truer than harrowing nightmares
it is the place I call home, my land, my living DMZ.

Playing at War

It is child's play atop the weather battered fortress
searching for an enemy in bright colors of summer.

Serious affairs come to terms on the fifth hour
as tea warms the chilled fingers of a winter's eve.

Over stilled bodies seasons pass in fresh morning grass
springs of life bathed in vermilion rivers
golden fires of burning pastures in fiery summers
the game remains in those growing hearts.

One by one they fall upon a bruised knee
scraping the gentle pain to make a noble pride.

It is child's play as they open those orbs upon the azure
a moment of awesome prayer for the grown brother.

Playing at life in the ruins of history
boys and girls shuffle their feet into the years
they hope for another instant of mutual warmth
as they collapse for a moment to the war they invented.

Plywood World

Another stormy night in their neighborhood
a warning came for twisters, hail, and fire
no one said anything about ghosts in the dark.

Eerie hours when the clocks have failed
and all seem to have stepped to the other side,
he finds himself looking for a way home.

But it was day and the light died somewhere above,
beyond the plywood windows of abandoned lives
silent and gray as if moved by the air of tombs.

He wonders, solitary in the shadows
whether these souls will assail him
trapped in prisons without addresses.

Nothing stirs, not a sparrow nor a wolf
the grass too is still after the heavy winds yet
close to the warmth of the offspring she dreams.

Every moment here is laden with black rains
homes ravaged by infernal flames
inhabitants frozen in a state of shock.

Boarded up fancies near frigid hearths
they are as cardboard boxes, as ancient citadels
to cast their threatening shadows upon the world.

Postcard Nevermore

How do you send notice from the underground,
apologize for forgetting a last goodbye
when the bones hang by a rotting thread?

He knows they look down to the dirt
seeking a last word from the one who could,
who had a way with a forgotten alphabet.

How do you write a will when you are out of ink
and your fingers have decayed into chalky coal
soon to be dust of the dust, mother of all worlds.

She wants to see the shores of unknown lands
longing for the images of charming seas
under scorching stars in the mist of Decembers.

But how does one send a postcard in a land of deserts
when the offices have closed millennium before
and the body is but a fog floating upon lost oceans?

Pray Little Girl, Pray

A dancer, as Degas may have once painted you
misty in a corridor bathed in a subtle light
you seem to waltz as you skip from tile to tile.

Not a sound, but a hazy envelope
surrounded by a dream, nothing could be more real,
eyes semi closed; a heart softly murmurs a praise.

Giddiness is not a question to be pondered
every fiber of your being floats in a tenuous dance
your dress shapes a skin of pearls, diamonds, and gold.

Your lips, your spirit, your breaths are a soft smile
gently your chest heaves a life you generously share
a gift few can comprehend, fewer are able to make.

Continue on your path little girl, a fall is unlikely
come closer, it seems the universe leads you forward
inexorably as it was meant to be when the world began.

You are a prayer answered, a prayer in the making;
no one knows whence your life force comes
pray little girl, pray, as you dance into tomorrow.

Remembering the Embrace

What does it take for the child
to receive the embrace of a frigid day?

He looks up to the sky for comfort;
the giant sees to a horizon so distant
forgetful of the offspring who needs a hand.

What does it take for a touch
stolen in the middle of mere dreams?

He knows a crowd of strangers surrounds
the days he lets unravel as the clock runs
unaware that tomorrow will steal their breaths.

What does it take for a breast
to be cupped in the palms of another?

He waits, roaming, almost invisible
as his infinite hopes continue to slowly beat
pleading at the rhythm of a lost beginning.

What does it take for that passion
to become free in the prison of fear?

He shivers in a shell crushed by the multitude
bruised by the punches of unknown foes
begging that the ache would give way to joy.

But what does it take to be seen
and received as a gift to the one in ashes?

Grooves upon a smile multiply to tell the tale
of a gentle spirit who dies under the anvil
his chest to brittles, at last he goes to sleep.

Renaissance Man

48

The surgeon
tireless with the scalpel
squinting to locate the pain
he cuts and heals.

The lumberjack
still cutting through
trunk and limb
planning for Winter long.

The welder
on his knees, facing the ark
a superhero making anew
scavenging the life, saver from death.

The gardener
a simple task, hoe in hand
scalping the weeds
saving lives surrounded with flowers.

The magician
everything he touches
smiles and inhales new life
into all, and the world smiles.

Sharing Wrinkles

I once held your hand of enthralling silk
caressed by the early light of a newly born world.

You recall the tall blades of mysterious grass
the refuge of those days of tender innocence.

We shared what they call youth in novels
a fantasy written upon a tombstone to be carved soon.

I saw the whispering of trembling hours
scribing their harsh embrace with a blunt knife.

You remained still with majestic stoicism
under the chisel of the unproven sculptor.

We fell to flashes of stars blinding the nights
their gentle sparks burning our breasts with fear.

I held your soul into my palms to make it safe
while the agony of life shocked every inch of you.

You opened your eyes with accepting despair
drowned in the sorrow of the upcoming storm.

We took another step under the leathery coat
ready to share our farewells beneath wrinkly flesh.

She Dreams

Little hands on the firm knees of enduring love
she pauses her spirit on the promise of the new sun.

Looking in the distance the ruby lips smile again
sighting a friend chasing the ball in the mist.

There will be no school for her, free she is yet
her cheek warm against the cozy lap of a mother.

Soon she will join in the plays of another everyday
but for now she listens to the hearty pulse beneath her ear.

Stabbed by the Ghosts

The ghosts know better than to
throw daggers into the air;
they polish their aim
and never miss a soft target.

The living alone may wonder
in the darkness of his night
whence the pain this day
has come on such swift wings.

The ghosts know to change the rain
to ice while they wave their spirits
their hellos of shallow misty breaths
slap on the chilled bones of their sons.

The living again stare into their space
puppets of a strange theater
they must be quiet in the ruckus
of those who once loved them.

The ghosts do know better than to
throw daggers into the air
young yet, they can only converse
with the frigid words of their dead pain.

Sunday Fog

Too early on a foggy Sunday
once again he sits on the curb.

Lights risk a shine upon the convenience store
it is still too soon to call it alive.

Surrounded by the cold aroma of a wet cigarette
his shaky hand attempts to light another.

The breath of a late night in the strip club
is like a glow in the November air.

He grins as he caresses the wide bandage
to keep the rainbow butterfly from an escape.

Yesterday yet he thought of a cubicle
making up stories for the weary callers.

Now he pondered as so many times before
the numbers to choose for a glorious end.

Alone for the hundredth time I spy a tear
too shy to risk being called his.

A colorful coat has turned gray,
from a distance I can guess his desire.

There is nothing left to purchase behind the gate
but stale beer and cheap cigarettes.

He recalls the days his father showed him
his voice failing, deep within a cancerous abyss.

Henry, he thinks but barely remembers his name
no one knows him anymore so "hon" will do.

Another drop and I see him shiver
today as every day for a thousand years.

The man sits on the curb by the convenience store
the grave he carefully digs with every sigh.

Terror in Town

They recall clouds of a heavy earth
snaking through the vales at high noon
and stopped in awe at the puzzling rage.

Behind the peeling wheel of that eerie race horse
resolved to another aimless journey
she bore a well-known frown as fixture.

When her kin sat in repose near wooden clogs
in ancient harmony as they contemplated the flight of the swallows
misunderstood, this devil sped through the meadow.

Chased by a taunting record of desolate tales
she never slowed to engage in a future
as the rust riddled carriage vanished in a sunless finale.

It was a little too early perhaps for a new sunrise
as she fitted the noose so tight
and vanished from memories as if she never was.

The Fun Thing about Dreaming

The skies fell on my abode
obscurity enveloped the realm at midday
and I ran for cover hungry for a vision.

What would it be on this journey,
a folly into subconscious paths
pursued by a reaper in creamy armor?

Perhaps a chance encounter with desire
a vaporous apparition in the shape of an ideal
close, yet so far to remain unattainable?

So many nights counted upon those walls
hoping for a glimpse into a gentle day
I dove faithful that all will be well.

When the appointed hour would ring
remained a terrifying proposition
at the gate of another unknown kingdom.

Illusory as the moment may be
so distant from the daily routines
its occurrence so uncertain it made it real.

Made from the matter of fulfilled fantasies
an ecstatic instant would become eternity
if only the storm continued forever.

Waltzing with the smile of angels at last
carried by the motion of infinite galaxies
I will treasure the tale in secret if I am to wake.

Ice Experiments

Freezing a joyful moment into an icy mirror
the dreamer seeks universality.

The idea into a found feather, the forgotten petal
as if sent into space to find its mate.

Potter spinning his wheel, the object turns
revealing infinity in sparks, spots and voids.

Letters from a lost encyclopedia, comic strip
they mix to project flashes of yellowed out sheets.

Dropping color, molten lava into the tiny ocean
to watch it become galaxies, a soundless big bang.

Closing those browns, the snapshot preserved
sleep is possible, deserved, full of needed memories.

Watch it decompose as he awakens to a broken ice age
dripping worlds, creations without master they live.

Alchemist of simple devices, father to the newborn
he can watch helpless universes form recklessly.

Frozen for an instant, observer of an experiment
now removed, it is time to share in the miracle.

To the Lake Running

The scream persists endlessly, carried on an infinite wave
little legs run, run little legs, you must escape
pursued by the giant lips, his eyes bulge ready to explode
little boy runs, and he wonders why.

His heart shrinks, as if caught in soiled plastic wrap
thrown at him by a vengeful hand but why?
little man runs... please run little man... do it for me
the knot is tighter, in his soul, with a sinking hope.

The look in those eyes, hate, anger, murderous gaze
little boy, cry... cry little boy... you know why
you forgot to forget; you too deserved a bit of living
the shame is yours; you should have known better.

Little Legs hurt... hurt little legs... that is why
alone, deal, do as you will, at seven, be a man now
to the lake, muddy, deep, full of your eternal sorrow
swim little man, little man swim, if you must, if you can.

Why the distorted beauty of her
the love temporary, gone, or perhaps to the tomb yet
the colossus could have been human, it runs faster
love little boy... little boy love... that is why.

The mouth gaping, hungry to swallow what it once made
image of a Hades dark, deep, cold, full of many deaths
little shorts, little shirt, little man, what did you do so?
Why, for... who else could it be?

Little boy into the waters... swim Little boy, little boy swim
it is safe now, the monster fears the wave
smile my buddy, my friend, my pal... together happy
little man... my dear friend... if only you could swim.

Your Crimson Tide

I want to be your crimson tide
to travel through you day and night
tease your soul with gentle notions
and warm your limbs with my sighs.

Into a syrup of honey and wine
I want to transform so you will dream
entranced with the mere juices of life
as I journey from your soul to your breast.

As if a babe in the womb, I will kick
and I will punch upon the walls of your veins
so you may sleep the peace of the righteous
indolent as a weary warrior in your alcove.

I will create maps to your every inch
to give you the keys to all your hidden secrets
so you may surrender to this life
and travel to our own impregnable worlds.

My body offered in effigy I will lie down
a domain to mimic your fancies within you
image of the little girl you once were
with every part, a ghost of your being.

And She Did Love Pretty Things, Really...

She hid so much kindness far within herself
screaming seemed to come more naturally to her
and she did love pretty things, really...

It was not a sweet tooth she had, but a mouthful;
impatience almost always got the better of her
and she could taste the savor in all things, really...

Her eyes captured nuances in hues and form
far too often she let the pain take over and win
but she knew beauty, and the delicateness around her.

Music was a sweet melody to those ears now silent
if only she had listened to the singing voices nearby
yet she was so inclined to recognize a symphony.

She left her mark, in little pieces of a loving one
so loud, so clear, on the minute world she left behind.
And she did love pretty things, really ...
                    and that she can no longer hide.

Piano on Saturn

Holding the wand like old Merlin
she is the conductor of galaxies
twirling through space as on first light.

She has played symphonies on every stage
audiences have stood for grand ovations
content invaded by sounds unknown in their parts.

Not the common prodigy in the world's orchestra
she has traveled to houses unknown, played
instruments made of mysterious fibers.

In all venues, her melodies mesmerized listeners
in ways none could begin to understand
as sounds permeated stratospheres near and far.

Virtuoso for all times she led orchestras to play
on Saturn as she had on Jupiter and on Mars
and would soon in Andromeda and other nebula.

Such enticing sounds she birthed
variations of a similar tune to hear the voice
of the universe naked in all its truths.

Immortal Dandies

It is 1920 in the city of dimming lights
fog has settled over a river thick with dark minds
slowing time to keep the little men safe
in the suits of old wealth, a cigarette burning
the fake delicateness between the stained digits.

A century has expired in the curb of false delights
the olive skin dandies continue to dream of
selves within the smoky clouds of their pretense
years others have died for a swirl in the air
as they remain frozen in their waxen bodies.

They yet have to change the world
grow into meaningful entities
if only they had the courage to exist
but they lie in the comfort of a daze
prefabricated by idle generations.

They might be models on the cover of glory
thin as the glossy paper made for fairy tales
hollow behind every word they once imagined
making revolutions by the hearth of a palace
now the laughingstock of the multitudes they once mocked.

Eternal Life For a Dime

They aimed at a heaven below through the dreams above
seeking to fulfill a promise of a life transcending in their hands
almighty travelers of science in fractions of numbers and signs.

They saw through infinite lenses, images of their many selves
magicians with steel tools rebuilding what had once seemed to die;
success became real when again they walked tall from the tomb.

They no longer strolled avenues of oaks, roses, and cherry blossoms
living off the stars, warm to the touch on hearts of icy blue metal
tastes of sweets, scents of oceans, all meaningless now.

Dogs howled at a friendlier moon while cats sought their friendship
once again alone with no hand to feed them or show them care
they took shelter in the palaces of those humans now departed.

Men reached a heaven below, wishing for a throne above
no more embracing, rather subsisting on eternity
now masters of a destiny beyond time, they stood stunned to life.

The Monk and the Anchoress

They watched in terrified awe as kin walked on
bowing before the idols of a maddened century.

She contemplated the loss of a father
shedding a tear at the recollection of his kind soul.

He attempted to refrain from the passion of hate
as monsters multiplied with stealthy speed.

They smiled as they shared the comforting thought
at least they felt close in the wish for a distant exile.

He, a monk, she, the anchoress, apart perhaps
yet inseparable by their common urge

They would run to the mountain tops
leaving behind the terror trail others follow.

Abandoned to a pure destiny with nothing
left to fear of man, free and away from a billion daggers.

Sparrows and Fireworks

Walking on forgotten asphalt
alone in the distance they attempt a smile
upon the hill yet yesterday a mob.

Gentle drops venture from above
chancing a journey among blinding rays
she wonders whether it will be sun or rain.

He offers a glance as she continues
thoughtful of the uncertain morrows
a faint sign of welcome in her eyes.

A vague siren screams down below
distracting a sparrow from its daily duties
but it persists in its call.

The field lives amid a dense forest
hoping to shake soon again
with the thunder of another fourth in July.

Data Dream

They dreamed of becoming gods in their day
tending to knowledge reserved for the infinite.

Hoping to shed the flesh they went to sleep
on the experimental slab of an uncertain fate.

In a maze of sugar-coated wires, they rested
trapped in a web made of multicolored strings.

The goal, an awakening to unlimited secrets
a little madness before loss of all senses.

The organic frame retracted upon the steel
as fresh features became an icy blue marble.

There they lay as some do on their final day
given to the universe hoping to belong.

But they did not know the cost of their demands
as now the citadel of their bodies fall into chaos.

The darkness of the unfathomable void
now afforded to the soul of the same matter.

What will remain of the ones who once were
sweet children on the playgrounds of birthing desires!

Yes, they aimed to break down the boundaries of life
seeking eternal selves beyond the matter of the earth.

But now they wither away in shocking convulsions
pray to what they could not see, or imagine.

Assailed from all parts by energies of innumerable stings
invaded in their whole by what they meant to achieve.

The fancy turned to nightmare as they slowly perish
tortured forevermore for their desperate attempt.

Soon none of who they once were will subsist
digested by that power they tried to capture.

Time and the City

The artist found it fanciful to film the city lights
on a Sunday morning when all yet slept.

She wondered what stories these flares might tell
as she sped the frames to write the tale.

Skies became fiery to celebrate another rise
of this terrifying star, bearer of life.

Comfortable within the palace of her years
far above the chaos she lives a new happiness.

Some say these are the same ideals repeated
as they began under Hellenistic skies.

She should know for she has journeyed
valiantly through so many eras.

A smirk ventures upon her magical lips for
she already understands what the book will tell.

Descendent of Olympus on the peaks of Gotham
she feels eternity in her infinite exile.

No one recognizes her in the urban space
timeless as her own domain.

The lights will continue their path to the edge
of the world she made forgotten of time.

Generations will perish under her watchful eye
faithful to a script prescribed before all things commenced.

Homeless in 2031

What a hardship it may be to carry
those wrinkles to the unavoidable hyper store
delaying the age of walking devices
to assist with steel when the flesh fails.

Practice makes perfect when one goes alone
decades with the leather gloves deep
in worn out jean pockets
a frown made for an ancient bronze.

She sees the masses passing in a blur for
they have not yet learned the art of a slow dance
to prepare for the great waltz with the stars
to them the quest for processed lives matters most.

Hands on an old quilt, repository of dynasties
she still sits on the front porch as
the paint peels and flies with the breeze
no one greets her in this deserted land.

Her thoughts are secret now, her eyes
fixed onto a miracle only she can discern
beyond the thinning envelope of her past
there seems to be little to attach this old soul.

Her suitcases are packed, piled in the dark corridor
her destination mysterious as it is certain
she will leave little behind but a shell of a house
carcass to be erased as if it had been built for ghosts.

Gnawing at the Flesh

Teeth gnaw at the flesh
hungry to erase what was once sweet.

There is a throbbing beating
at the rhythm of a slowing heart.

It feeds to grow like a playing ball
made of rebar and concrete.

The creature has no game in mind
its only purpose to wreck a world.

With glowing eyes, it seeks another target
red with fire it burns like a venomous reptile.

It dreams of many kin for a great invasion
to overtake the domain of the formerly young.

Showing the way to an army of demons
it follows veins, arteries, and crevasses.

It devours the hopes and deeds of the kind spirit
until it too, in a senseless act, faces its own demise.

Summer Like a Dress

She wears the seasons as would a painter
a-temporal with every passing present.

I remember reflecting the darkness of winter
upon the somber coat so fitting to the maiden
little girl she may have been in her latter hours.

Wrapped within her warming hopes
she just stepped from the last colors of fall
bearing the aura of those tender musky memories
tumbled with the corpses of a dying spring.

She seems not to fear the hazards of the city
a silky skin mildly shaping her own curves
she strolls oblivious to the haunting moans.

Today it is a light gray sky floating near her breast
on a walk to rest, she might be dancing without time.

101st Street Bridge Tenant

Sitting on the edge of his freshly cut Bermuda
he waves uncertain hellos to the drivers
speaking inaudible phrases to who may hear him.

Nearby his home of steel on wheels
within his reach reassures him a little,
his possessions within his fearful gaze.

Thin plastic bags bearing odd coats of arms
from this fancy market and that discount store
protect treasures he alone can value.

Tonight, he will dream in black and white
recalling schooldays perhaps not his own
a home of brick or wood by a stream, but whose?

I know just one thing about him who hides
behind the reckless hair like a mane
he exists under the bridge as lives speed by.

Still, he will remain, when awake again
he will roll in a faded, camouflaged sleeping bag
to ready for a new day as if his open-air suite was palatial.

73

AUTHOR PROFILE

Fabrice Poussin teaches French and English at Shorter University. Author of novels and poetry, his work has appeared in Kestrel, Symposium, The Chimes, and many other magazines. His photography has been published in The Front Porch Review, the San Pedro River Review as well as other publications. In August 2021, his collection "In Absentia," was published by Silver Bow.